LEGO® CITY

READER COLLECTION
6 EASY-TO-READ STORIES

LEGO CITY — LEVEL 1
HELP IS ON THE WAY!
By Sonia Sander
■SCHOLASTIC

LEGO CITY — LEVEL 1
CALLING ALL CARS!
N: 50380
POLICE
By Sonia Sander
■SCHOLASTIC

LEGO CITY — LEVEL 1
READY FOR TAKEOFF!
By Sonia Sander
■SCHOLASTIC

LEGO CITY — LEVEL 1
FIRE TRUCK TO THE RESCUE!
By Sonia Sander
■SCHOLASTIC

LEGO CITY — LEVEL 1
ALL ABOARD!
By Sonia Sander
■SCHOLASTIC

LEGO MEDIEVAL ADVENTURES — LEVEL 2
Troll Attack
■SCHOLASTIC

SCHOLASTIC INC.

NEW YORK   TORONTO   LONDON   AUCKLAND

SYDNEY   MEXICO CITY   NEW DELHI   HONG KONG

HELP IS ON THE WAY!

By Sonia Sander

LEGO® City: Help is on the Way! (978-0-545-15068-2) © 2009 The LEGO Group. LEGO® City: Calling All Cars! (978-0-545-15523-6) © 2010 The LEGO Group. LEGO® City: Ready for Takeoff! (978-0-545-21986-0) © 2010 The LEGO Group. LEGO® City: Fire Truck to the Rescue! (978-0-545-11543-8) © 2009 The LEGO Group. LEGO® City: All Aboard! (978-0-545-17764-1) © 2010 The LEGO Group. LEGO, the LEGO logo, the Brick and the Knob configurations and the Minifigure are trademarks of the LEGO Group.

© 2011 The LEGO Group. Produced by Scholastic Inc. under license from the LEGO Group.

Published by Scholastic Inc. SCHOLASTIC and associated logos are trademarks and/or registered trademarks of Scholastic Inc.

This collection first printing, March 2011

ISBN 978-0-545-35799-9

12 11 10 9 8 7 6 5 4   13 14 15 16/0

46

Printed in Singapore
Scholastic, Inc.
557 Broadway
New York, NY 10012

Bear walks Jessie to school.
He barks at the cars as they cross.
Woof! Woof!
Beep! Beep!

But he hasn't.
No one Jesse asks has seen Bear.
Oh, no, poor Bear is lost.

Jessie hears Bear cry.
She finds him in the park.
Poor Bear is stuck under a gate!

Bear needs help fast.
Jessie asks the police for help.

Bear needs to be dug out.
The police call in even more help.

C-r-r-r-e-e-a-a-k-k!
Jessie's new friends lift
the gate off Bear.

The workers take good care of Bear.
They wrap up his paw.

28

LEGO CITY

CALLING ALL CARS!

N: 50380

50380

POLICE

By Sonia Sander
Illustrated by Mada Design

They speed off in a van.
Z-o-o-o-m!

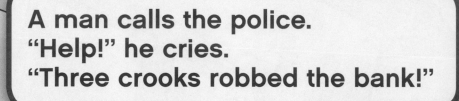

A man calls the police.
"Help!" he cries.
"Three crooks robbed the bank!"

The police race to the bank. Lights flash and sirens blare.

BANK

POLICE

POLICE

The police look for clues.
They watch the bank video.

Outside, the police ask questions. They find out about the van.

45

The police study the clues.
Now they know who to look for.
They will look for a red van.

An officer spots the van.
"Calling all cars," he says.
"I found the crooks.
I need backup fast!"

The police car follows the van.
Woo-ooh! Woo-ooh!
The chase is on!

S-c-r-e-e-e-c-h!
The police block the van.
The crooks are trapped.

"Freeze!" yell the police.
"Put your hands in the air!"
The police arrest the crooks.

The police look in the van.
They find the money.

The crooks go to jail. *Slam!*

LEGO® CITY
READY FOR TAKEOFF!

By Sonia Sander
Illustrated by Mada Design

GATES
A1-A3
←

GATES
B1-B3
↑

GATES
C1-C3
→

Where is the gate?

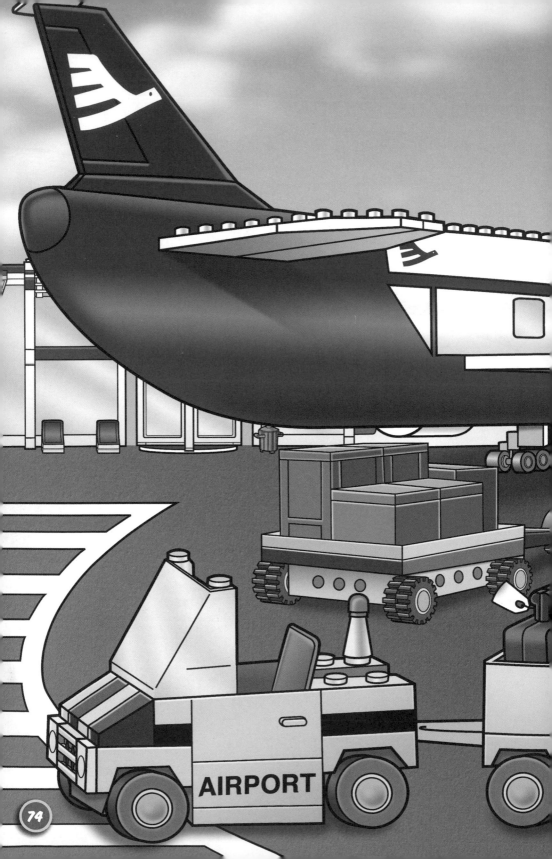

They fill the plane with gas.

The pilot is ready in the cockpit.
The ground crew shows
the pilot where to go.

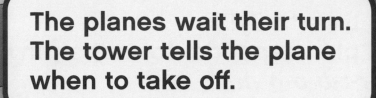

The planes wait their turn. The tower tells the plane when to take off.

It is time to fly!
The plane speeds down the runway.
V-r-r-r-o-o-o-m!

The plane flies into the sky.
It soars above the clouds.

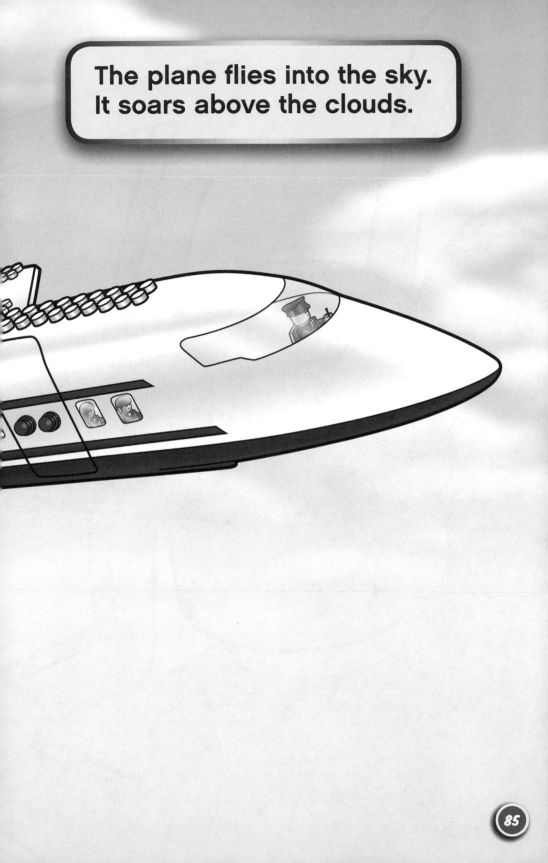

Look out the window.
See how small the city looks.

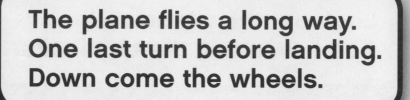

The plane flies a long way.
One last turn before landing.
Down come the wheels.

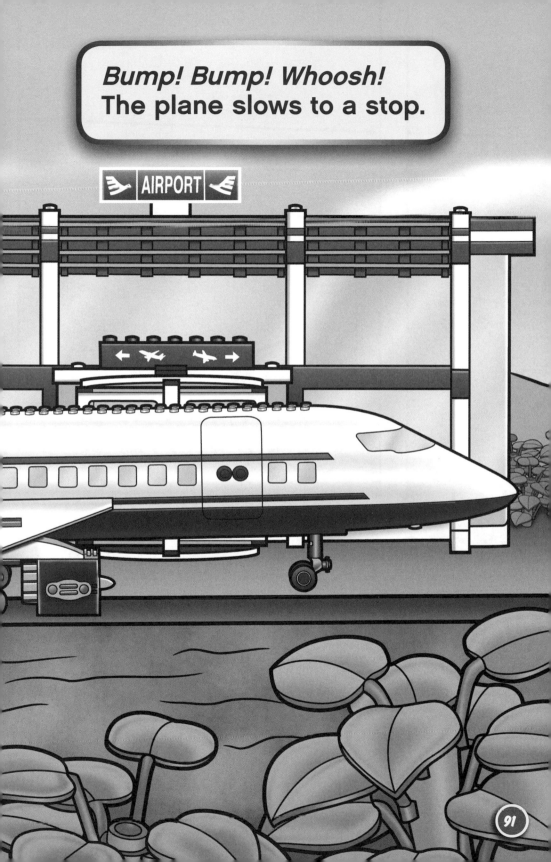

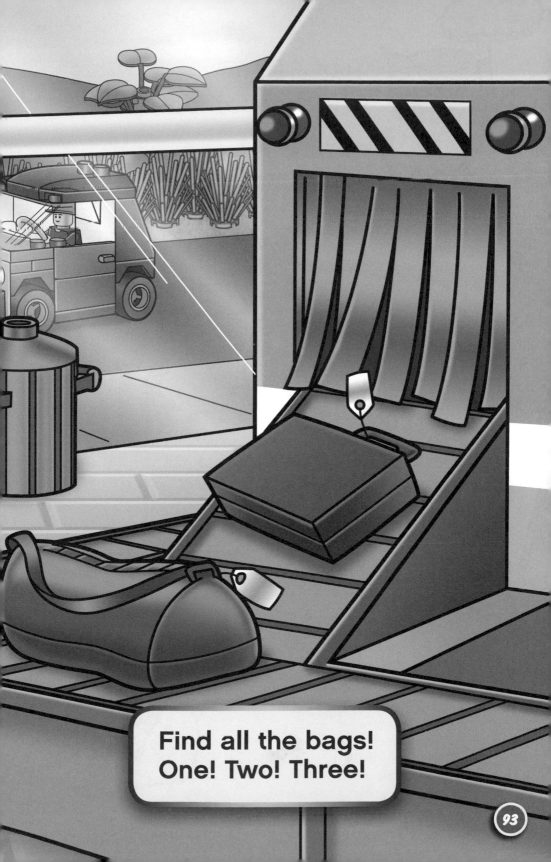

Find all the bags!
One! Two! Three!

Oh no!
Smoke is in the air.
There is a fire in the city.

Call 911 right away!
The firefighters can save the day.

B-r-r-r-i-i-i-n-g!
The fire alarm rings.
The firefighters are on their way.

One by one, they jump into action.
They slide down the pole.

The firefighters dress in a flash.
They grab their hats and boots.

V-r-o-o-o-m! V-r-o-o-o-m!
The fire truck is ready to go.

W-o-o-o-o! Honk! Honk!
The fire truck races down the road.

There is no time to lose.
It is time to fight the fire!

Bang! Crash!
Break down the door.
Go fight the fire.

Meow! Meow!
Up goes the ladder. One brave firefighter saves the cat.

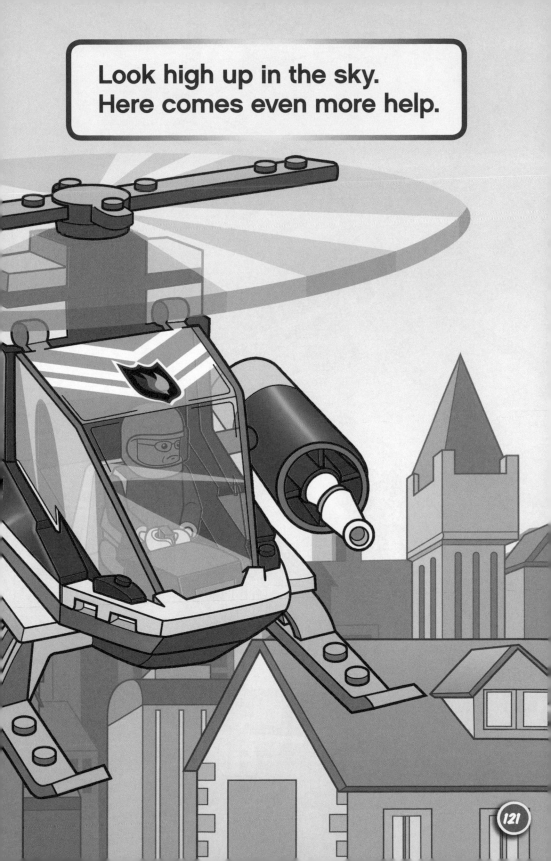

Look high up in the sky.
Here comes even more help.

Water sprays all over.
The fire starts to die down.

At last the fire is out.
The tired firefighters head home.

It has been a very long day.
The firehouse is quiet for now.
Only a few soft snores can be heard.

LEGO CITY

ALL ABOARD!

By Sonia Sander

It is time for the train to get to work.

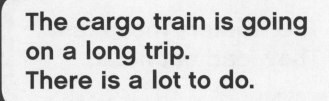

The cargo train is going
on a long trip.
There is a lot to do.

The workers move fast.
They load each car.

The train races over the track.
Click-clack! Click-clack!

The train runs all day long.
It goes up and down hills.

The train runs all night long.
It goes in and out of big cities.

7939

The train passes farms, too.
The cows say hello.
Moooo!

The train pulls into the station. It is right on time.

155

One by one, the cars are unloaded.

The job is almost done.

Now it is time to clean up.
The cargo train had a long trip.
It will be ready to go again soon.

LEGO Medieval ADVENTURES

Troll  Attack

By Allison Lassieur
Illustrated by Mada Design, Inc.

"Take that, troll!"

Sir Gavin swung his sword at the troll in front of him. *BAM!* The troll was knocked to the ground. Another green troll rushed forward. Sir Gavin attacked. Soon the troll ran away.

The battle was over. Sir Gavin grinned. King Edward's army had won the battle against the evil wizard Morax and his troll army!

King Edward rode his horse onto the battlefield. The knights gathered around him. "Hooray for King Edward!" shouted the knights.

"Morax sent his trolls to capture the castle," King Edward said. "Once again, he is defeated!"

Suddenly a burst of light and smoke filled the battlefield. The evil wizard appeared.

"I have not lost," Morax shouted. "My army will return, and you will lose!" *CRACK!* Morax disappeared.

King Edward looked at his knights. "We must find out when the troll army will attack," he said worriedly. "Who will volunteer for this dangerous mission?"
"I will!" Sir Gavin shouted.

"You must go into the Forbidden Forest," said the king. "Find out when and where the troll army will attack. Then report back to me."

"I won't fail," Sir Gavin said, bowing.

"Look for help near the Shadow Caves," the king said mysteriously.

Sir Gavin rode deep into the Forbidden Forest. The forest was dim and stuffy. No birds sang. Nothing moved.

The knight searched the forest for any signs of
the troll army. He looked near the Scary Swamp.

He searched the Gloomy Grove.

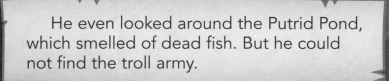

He even looked around the Putrid Pond, which smelled of dead fish. But he could not find the troll army.

Sir Gavin was discouraged. He did not want to fail King Edward. Then he remembered what the king had said about the Shadow Caves.

"What help can I possibly find there?" Sir Gavin said to himself. But he rode toward the caves anyway.

When he arrived, it was night. *It's too dark to search the caves,* Sir Gavin thought. *I will look in the morning.*

Suddenly a twig snapped. Sir Gavin drew his sword. "Who is there?" he shouted. "Speak!"

A cloaked figure stepped out of the shadows.

"Who are you?" Sir Gavin said.

The figure lifted the hood.

"Princess Alyssa!" Sir Gavin exclaimed. "I don't believe it!"

Princess Alyssa smiled. "Yes, it's me," she said.

Princess Alyssa and Sir Gavin sat down.
"I thought you were Morax's prisoner," Sir Gavin said.
"I have found a way to escape," Princess Alyssa said.
"Then why don't you?" Sir Gavin asked.
"This way," she said, "I can find out what he is up to."
"You are a spy!" Sir Gavin said.
The princess laughed. "Father doesn't want anyone to know," she said. "He must trust you very much."

Sir Gavin glowed with pride. "Do you have any news?" he asked.

"Yes," the princess said. "The troll army will attack at sunrise. And Morax is sending giant trolls."

Giant trolls! They were huge and strong. None of the king's weapons could defeat a giant troll.

"That is bad news," Sir Gavin said. He jumped up. "I must warn the king at once."

"Wait," the princess said.

She gave Sir Gavin a glass bottle filled with a blue liquid.

"This is a sleeping potion," she said. "I took it from Morax's workroom. A few drops will put a person to sleep."

"Does it work on trolls?" Sir Gavin asked.

"I don't know," Princess Alyssa said.

The princess pulled the hood over her face. "I must get back before the guards notice I am gone. Good luck!" She disappeared into the forest.

Sir Gavin raced back to the castle. When he arrived he went straight to the king. He gave the potion to the king. He told King Edward about meeting the princess.

"My daughter is smart and brave," King Edward said proudly. "I hope her plan works."

By sunrise everything was ready. The king and his knights stood along the castle walls. Large catapults stood ready to shoot huge boulders at the troll army. "I hope this works," Gavin said.

A low rumble sounded in the distance. It grew louder. It was the troll army! Gavin gripped his sword. Sure enough, there were several giant trolls with the army. The massive army marched to the castle gate.

Suddenly a loud *CRACK!* filled the air. The evil wizard Morax appeared.

"Prepare to meet your doom!" he shouted at the king.

King Edward smiled. "We shall see," he said.

"Fire the catapults!" the king shouted. Several huge boulders flew through the air toward the troll army.

The giant trolls marched forward. One by one, they swung their clubs at the boulders. *BAM! BAM! BAM!* The boulders shattered like glass.

Morax laughed. "See!" he said. "You cannot defeat my army! The castle will be mine!"

A strange blue smoke rose from each piece of stone. Soon the battlefield was covered in blue fog.

One by one, the trolls sank to the ground. They began to snore. The giant trolls crashed to the ground. Their snoring was so loud that the castle walls shook.

ZZZZ

"Get up!" Morax shouted. He poked a giant troll with his staff. The troll yawned and rolled over. "Get up, I say!" Morax screamed. But it was too late.

"This is not over!" Morax said furiously. He waved his staff. The whole army disappeared with a *WHOOSH*. Then with a *CRACK!* Morax disappeared, too.

The king's army began to cheer. "Hooray!" shouted Sir Gavin.

"Well done, Sir Gavin," King Edward said. "We have defeated Morax once again, thanks to you and Princess Alyssa."